Best Kind of Baby

Kate Laing • *pictures by* R. W. Alley

Dial Books for Young Readers New York

To Polly S. Brooks—"Big Granny" —K. L.
For big sister Cassie and little brother Max —R. W. A.

Published by Dial Books for Young Readers
A division of Penguin Putnam Inc.
345 Hudson Street • New York, New York 10014

Text copyright © 2003 by Kate Laing
Pictures copyright © 2003 by R. W. Alley
All rights reserved • Designed by Nancy R. Leo-Kelly
Text set in Stempel Schneidler
Manufactured in China on acid-free paper
10 9 8 7 6 5 4 3 2 1

Library of Congress Cataloging-in-Publication Data
Laing, Kate.
Best kind of baby / by Kate Laing ; pictures by R. W. Alley.
p.   cm.
Summary: When her parents tell her that her mother is expecting
a baby, Sophie imagines that she will have a baby mouse or puppy
or monkey or dolphin.
ISBN 0-8037-2662-7
[1. Babies—Fiction. 2. Imagination—Fiction. 3. Brothers and
sisters—Fiction.] I. Alley, R. W. (Robert W.), ill. II. Title.
PZ7.L1575 So 2003   [E]—dc21   2001053729

The full-color artwork was prepared using watercolor and pencil.
Sophie's drawings are by Max Alley.

One day Sophie was feeding Pretty Pink Princess raspberry jam when her parents came into the room.

"Sophie," said her mommy, "we have the most wonderful news! We are going to have a baby!"

"Isn't that exciting?" said her daddy. "Aren't you happy to be getting a little brother or sister?"

Sophie looked at her doll. She put Pretty Pink Princess in the very back of her closet.

"Can we have pizza for dinner?" she asked.

That night Sophie's mommy and daddy took her and her best friend Phoebe out for her favorite dinner.

"Why is your mommy eating so much pizza?" asked Phoebe.

"She needs lots of cheese because she's going to have a little baby mouse," Sophie explained.

"After it's born, we'll chew tunnels in the walls, tease the cat, and nibble on everyone's toes."

"It doesn't look like a mouse to me," said Phoebe.

"Sophie, honey," laughed her mother, "you know that we are going to have a human baby, not a little mouse!"

"Squeak, squeak," said Sophie.

One hot afternoon Sophie's other best friend Nicky came over. They made super-duper sundaes with whipped cream, hot fudge, and cherries on top.

"Is your mommy eating too many sundaes?" asked Nicky. "You're not supposed to have more than five or six a day."

"Mommy's tummy is getting so big because she's having a little baby puppy," Sophie explained.

"When it's born, we'll play fetch, roll in all the mud puddles, and bark at the mailman!"

"Can I play with it too?" asked Nicky.

"Sophie, sweetie," said her daddy, smiling, "Mommy's not having a puppy. We already have a dog. You're going to have a little brother or sister."

"Woof, woof," said Sophie.

"Slurp," said the dog.

One sunny fall day Sophie was climbing on the
jungle gym with her almost best friend Libby.

"Your mommy looks like she swallowed a basketball!" said Libby. "How did she do that?"

"It's not a basketball," Sophie explained. "It's a little baby monkey. After it's born, we're going to eat bananas, swing through the trees, and throw coconuts at everyone."

"I want a little baby monkey too!" wailed Libby.

"Sophie, my silly," said her mommy, "we are not having a baby monkey. Monkeys are wild animals. You are going to be a big sister to a lovely little boy or girl."

"Ee-ee-oo-oo," said Sophie.

At nursery school pickup, Sophie's fourth best friend Avery said, "Your mommy looks funny. She can't even button her coat. She's like a huge, huge whale!"

"Nope," said Sophie, "not a whale. Mommy's having a little baby dolphin. After it's born, we're going to leap through the waves, dive way, way down, and then zoom back up and spray water all over everyone!"

"Can I come too?" asked Avery.

"Sophie," said her mother, "I'm not having a dolphin. Dolphins live in the ocean. We live in a house. We are having a baby. A little baby human child."

Sophie put her head in her cubby. "Splash, splash," she said softly.

Then one day it wasn't Sophie's mommy who came to pick her up at nursery school.

"Daddy's here!" yelled Sophie. She looked around. "Where's Mommy?"

"We're going to see her now," said her daddy.
"She's at the hospital and she can't wait to see you!"

They drove to a shiny white building.

Inside, Sophie and her father walked past a room with lots of babies. Sophie looked and looked but she didn't see any baby mice or dogs or monkeys or dolphins, not anywhere.

But in another big
room there were lots of
mommies lying in beds.

"There's my mommy!"
Sophie ran over and gave
her a huge kiss.

"Where did your tummy
go?" asked Sophie.

"It's right here on my
lap," said her mother. "It's
a little baby brother. His
name is Sammy."

"What does it do?" asked Sophie.

"Not very much yet," said her mother. "But you're his big sister, so you can teach him lots of things."

"Hmmm," said Sophie. She looked at the baby brother. He was drooling. *Kind of like a puppy,* thought Sophie.

"I guess I could teach him how to play catch," she said.

Sophie looked again, a little closer this time. The baby went *"Urp, pllllzzzz,"* and the drool sprayed up into the air. *Kind of like a dolphin,* thought Sophie.

"I could maybe teach him how to swim," she said.

Sophie peeked under the baby's blanket. His arms and legs were waving all around. *Kind of like a monkey,* Sophie thought.

"He'll have to learn how to climb trees. I know I could teach him that."

"Eek! Goo-squeak!" said the baby.
"That means he's hungry," said her mother.
Probably for cheese, thought Sophie.

"I'll have to show him how to eat pizza without all the cheese falling off too," said Sophie. "You know, he's kind of like a puppy and a dolphin and a monkey and a mouse all at the same time!"

Sophie's parents looked at Sammy.

"I guess that he is!" said her daddy.

And then the little baby smiled—right at Sophie.

"Oooh-coo-gur-gle," said the little baby.

He might even be . . . thought Sophie, *a little bit . . . better.*